Stardust

Catherine Prutton

DEDICATION

For James and Harry

CONTENTS

ACKNOWLEDGMENTS

Thank you to everyone who has encouraged and believed in me and my poems, and to anyone who has liked, shared, bought or read them. Thank you to those who have helped me pull this collection together.

STARDUST

There's a secret up there in the stars,
listen closely and you'll hear it,
some of us already know
but not everyone believes it.

But we are made of stardust
we're bursting at the seams,
with cosmic dust that fills us up
with magic while we dream.

It's just beneath the surface,
it glistens on our lips,
it lingers in our footprints
and it drips from fingertips.

Just think of what could happen,
imagine if you knew!
That all the magic you'll ever need
is right there, inside of you.

MAGIC IN THE STARS

There is magic in the stars
if you look really hard,
and the moon holds secrets
you can keep in a jar,

and clouds collect dreams
that burst from the seams,
and the sun drops wishes
on your head with its beams.

And planets cast spells
that make your heart swell,
and comets shower potions
to fill up the wishing wells.

So when you can see the magic
and you feel a little blue,
just look up and it's there
waiting patiently for you.

CAPTURING BEAUTY

And just like the moon
her beauty refused
to be captured
by lens or zoom,

no camera could capture,
no image replicate,
her nuance and beauty
visible only by gaze.

When finally they realised
pictures only misled,
they had no choice
but to bask in her light instead.

SILENT GROWTH

When did the trees get so big?
Why did I not see
the transformation
from seed to tree,
when it was happening
all the while
right in front of me?
Why only now
when stood tall and proud,
do I finally see
its journey
from the ground?
That silent growth,
unseen by most
takes us one day
by surprise.
And if, despite
unseeing eyes
they can spread their limbs
towards the sky
then so can you,
and so can I.

NO SEED, NO SHOOT

Sow the seeds
the plants will grow,
if you don't try
you'll never know,

and though it won't
be guaranteed
that life will grow
from every seed,
the ones that do
will thrive,
you'll see,

no seed, no shoot,
no shoot, no tree.

BLOOM

When a flower
fails to bloom
we do not chastise,
we ask ourselves
why it's unable
to thrive.
We're patient,
we're kind,
give it space,
give it time.
Imagine then
if we applied
the same
love and kindness
to you
and to I.
Oh my.

DANDELION

I picked myself a dandelion,
held up to my lips and blew,
I closed my eyes and made a wish
and on the breeze it flew.

That ordinary dandelion,
had grown through mud and cracks,
had found its way through darkness
finding light on strange new paths.

And now I wished upon it
in an act of joy and hope,
proof enough that even in the darkness
beauty grows.

MAGNOLIA

The sun will set,
the moon will rise,
the stars will always shine.

The magnolia
will bloom again
and so will you,
in time.

SAIL

When calm seas
give way to gales,
when your engine
starts to fail,

before you quit,
before you bail,
do not fret -
adjust your sails.

Ride the waves,
sail with the tide,
let your instinct
be your guide,

the stormy waves
will soon subside,
to calmer seas
and clearer skies.

ROUGH SEAS

In rough seas
we learn to sail,
we find the light
when dark prevails,
rebuild again after the gale.
We try, we trip,
we fall, we fail,
we rise and live to tell the tale.

MAYBE TOMORROW

Maybe tomorrow,
or the day after,
in a week,
a month
or two,
things will change
and get better,
remember this –
they *always* do.
Sometimes,
the only way out
is through.

THIS PART WILL END

I know it's hard,
I know it's tough,
I know you're done
you've had enough.

But stick it out
and things will change,
nothing ever stays
the same.

Good days are close,
just round the bend,
don't give up now,
this part will end.

DAWN

When you're tired
and feeling worn,
when your heart
is bruised and torn,

just remember
that the night
is always darkest
before the dawn.

RESCUE

I thought someone
was coming to rescue me,
but it turns out I was wrong,

the person I needed
to save me was me,
and I'd been there
all along.

FOOLISH

Foolish of me
to believe
that what I need
is out of reach,

when really
all I need
is already
inside of me.

SHE LET GO

She let go
of everything
she thought
she had to be,

and with nothing left
to tie her down
finally,
she was free.

MY NEIGHBOURS' LAWN

My neighbours' lawn
was plush and soft,
seemed never to succumb
to the cold and frost.

My own lawn was fine
but theirs so much better -
the flowers stood proud,
so neat, so together!

I racked my brains,
how could it be?
Just how did they get it
so lush and so green?

I ignored my own lawn
drove myself almost mad
wondering how I could
have what they had -

I wasted so much time frowning
and scratching my head
that my own flowers withered,
and my grass is now dead.

SHOES

I was jealous of your shoes,
jealous of their shine and jewels,
of how you walked so sure and tall
whilst in my own I'd trip and fall.

I tried them on for size and feel,
they pinched my toes and rubbed my heels
and all the while you'd kept your pace,
no trace of pain across your face.

No good arrives when we compare
our own shoes to another pair,
unless you've tried do not assume
how it feels to walk in someone else's shoes.

DRY AGAIN

Do not be afraid
of the pain
or the rain,
both are good for growth
and neither of them stay,
the clouds will come and go
and you'll soon
be dry again.

TAKE MY HAND

I don't have all the answers,
I don't know what to say,
I don't know why this happened
or how long you'll feel this way,

but if you need me take my hand
I'll guide you through the dark,
or I'll sit with you and wait
until it's light enough to start.

I WAS WRONG

I'm sorry for saying
you're so strong,
I was wrong.

Instead
I should have said
here let me,
that looks heavy,

let me carry it
for a while,
and I'll be here
when you're ready.

CHANGE

Change is the only constant in life, and resisting it is like trying to hold back the tide with your hands. You may be able to keep hold of a small amount of water for a short while, but you'll be too afraid to move in case you spill any, and you'll be so focused on what's in your hands that you'll miss what the new tide brings. Let go. Who knows what will wash up on the shore.

IT MATTERS

All of it matters, all of it. It matters because you made it matter. You took this strange and wonderful experience and you made something of it. You loved and tried and failed and tried again. Your very existence has created ripples that will continue forever. You've touched lives and your existence has changed the trajectory of those around you. You existed, you know it and I know it. Right here, right now, and that's what counts.

PLODDING

I'd like to state my case for plodding (hear me out); plodding is misunderstood, there's nothing exciting about plodding. But sometimes, it's the only option. Plodding says 'I'm still going, I'm still here, I'm just going at my own pace.' It's the courage to say 'You go ahead, I'll meet you at the top, I might be going slowly right now but at least I haven't stopped.'

TINY STEPS

What if you did that thing you think would make you happier? What if you did just one thing today that would bring you closer to it, and what if you did another thing tomorrow to bring you closer still? And what if you carried on until you're eventually doing the thing that would make you happier? Think of how proud you would be for investing in yourself. Don't be put off by the amount of time it will take, the time will pass anyway. Be brave, take a step - even if it's tiny, it will get you started. Tiny steps add up and before you know it, you'll be half way there.

COURAGE

It takes much courage
and bravery
to say this path
is no longer for me,

to decide it's time
to take control,
to try new paths
and set new goals,

to take hold of
the reins of your life
and say -
this is where I decide
to go today.

How brave you are,
to steer your ship towards the stars,
and decide it's never too late
for a brand new start.

RIPPLES

Drop kindness
like a pebble
into every
single river,

the ripples will
grow and spread
and reach again
the giver.

Drop enough,
and you will find
one day
eventually,

kindness will find
its way to
someone stranded
in the sea.

IT'S OKAY

It's okay
to lose your way,
to try one path
and then turn back,
to find yourself
down one road
then decide it's not
the way you want to go.
It's okay to say
this is not for me,
there's somewhere else
I'd rather be.
It's okay to try,
it's okay to fail,
to lose it all
and start again.
It's okay to stumble and trip
along the twists
and turns and bends,
we all end up
where we're meant to be
anyway,
in the end.

MIGRATION

A change in the air
and away they fly,
to calmer seas
and warmer climes,

so too can we
say our goodbyes
to find a better
place to thrive,

beyond the horizon
there's more you'll see,
spread your wings,
set yourself free.

WONDERING

If you're wondering
where to find me,
I'll tell you
where I'll be,

I'm in that in-between bit,
that space where
sky meets sea.

In the whispers
of the trees
and the edges
of your dreams,

close enough to
almost touch but
slightly out of reach.

I'm in the moon
and in the stars
but never really far,

and always, always,
I'm there, inside
your heart.

WHERE DID YOU GO?

Where did you go?
I often wonder.
The space that you
took up so completely
can't just be gone forever?
Afterwards, I searched
for something to remind
me of you,
a tangible object
I would inevitably lose,
that would leave me
disappointed
because it wasn't
actually you.
But then, I see you
smiling in my dreams
and hear your laughter
on the breeze,
and you're so alive
in my memories
that I realise,
you didn't ever
really leave.

SMASHED TO PIECES

When your life
has smashed to pieces,
scattered fragments
in the dirt,

when the life
you thought you knew
is now the cause
of pain and hurt,

pick up those tiny pieces
and make a brand new start,
a mosaic of your memories
now a beautiful work of art.

Fill the gaps with love and joy
and revel in its glory,
each piece now a reminder
you had the courage
to change your story.

DISCO BALL

Behold the majestic disco ball,
brings light and joy
to one and all,
look closer though
and you will see
a story in each broken piece.
A tale of strength
and hope and grit,
how she glued herself back again
bit by bit,
and underneath her
now we dance,
we celebrate
her second chance.
Next time you're
shattered from a fall
remember –
you're not broken,
you're a goddamn
disco ball!

YOU ARE STILL HERE

We know the trees still exist
when fog persists
and will not clear,
so when it descends
upon our heads
and threatens to make us
disappear,
remember -
just like
the trees,
you are still here,
you are still here.

HAPPY ENOUGH

Happiness should not be the only goal,
we need resilience to tread this road.
Courage to carry on
when things get tough,
and to find the joy
when the going gets rough.
The faith to know that
despite the dreadful days,
brighter ones are on their way.
To dust ourselves off
after a fall,
and be happy enough,
in spite of it all.

JOY

Some find joy elusive,
scarce or hard to find,
spend a lifetime looking up,
around, below, behind.

But joy is never hiding,
though it's often overlooked,
it's in the perfect cup of tea
or in the pages of a book.

In small forgotten places,
gestures not always grand,
a shared smile with a stranger
or a friend who understands.

It's closer than you think,
it's in the crannies and the nooks,
just waiting to be discovered
once you realise where to look.

WASHING LINE

The t-shirts on the washing line
get bigger every year,
sails upon a ship whose course
I can no longer steer.

I peg each one out slowly
as if to stall the time,
try not to think of how one day
they won't be on my line.

And though the days are often long
the years fly by so fast,
by the time I've stopped to catch my breath
another one has passed.

But for now I pause
as I take in this fleeting view,
I close my eyes and soak it up,
the shirts, the sun and you.

FEET

It wasn't so long ago
your feet lay neatly
in my palm,

those tiny toes
I'd stare at
as you slept
within my arms.

But now the moments
that I catch your feet
are few and far between,

someday perhaps
they'll walk on paths
that I have never been,

and walk upon exotic sands
in far off foreign lands,
but for just a moment longer
let me hold them
in my hands.

CONKERS

The conker shells are sprouting
and it takes me by surprise,
autumn seems so far away
in the warm heat of July.

Their spikey cases juxtaposed
against the summer haze,
I'd forgotten all about
the cooler breeze, the shorter days.

A gentle but firm reminder
they whisper as they sway -
remember change is on the way,
change is always on the way.

MAYBE YESTERDAY

Maybe yesterday
you moved mountains,
perhaps tomorrow
you'll feel
less inclined,
and whichever
you choose
to do today
is absolutely fine.

NEXT STEP

If the road
is feeling long
and you're feeling
out of breath,

don't think about
the mountain,
just take the
next step.

MOUNTAIN VIEW

The journey
feels tough sometimes,
I know –
I feel it too,
but if we don't
climb the
mountain
we won't
see the view.

HEAL

That wound that feels
so raw, so exposed,
will soon heal
if left alone.
Your intuition feels,
it knows,
the direction it needs to go
to grow.
Eventually it will be
less sore, less tender,
and only when you look
will you remember
how far you've come,
how you survived,
and afterwards
how you flew,
how you thrived.

RIDICULOUS LIFE

If life feels a bit ridiculous,
it's probably because it is,
when it seems to make
no sense at all, my friend
consider this –

we're spinning on a planet
that is floating out in space,
and seemingly from nowhere
sprang an entire human race,

and someday soon
not far from now
we'll all cease to exist,

so what else to do
but celebrate
the here, the now,
the this.

EMBRACE IT ALL

The days are long,
the years are fast,
tomorrow will soon
be in the past.

Forgive, forget,
move on and grow,
release the old
and let it go.

The good, the bad,
the rise and fall
lean in, arms wide,
embrace it all.

LOVE IN LARGE AMOUNTS

We can dream about tomorrow
and reminisce about yesterday,
we can make plans for the future
but they can soon be snatched away,

and sometimes we're reminded
of what really, really counts -
courage, strength, compassion, hope
and love in large amounts.

SUCCESS

I used to think success
was trying to impress,
striving for the best
and expecting nothing less.

But now I know success
is a warm hand to caress,
giving more, expecting less
and counting ways in which
I'm blessed.

REST

I had hit a wall
and though my journey stalled,
I realised that upon it
I could sit,
rest my mind
and legs a bit,
until my breath
was steady
and I was feeling ready
to try and climb
over it.

HOME

I've finally
figured it out,
after searching
near and far,
that home can be
anywhere,
but it's always
where you are.

WHAT ARE THE CHANCES?

Tell me, what are the chances?
I couldn't possibly calculate.
The reason for us being here
I will forever contemplate.

I could think on it forever
and still not understand how,
but I'm so glad to be existing
here with you, right now.

ROLLERCOASTER

They told us love should be a rollercoaster,
fast and full of thrills,
that it didn't count unless it made you scream
or made you ill.

And yes, sometimes it's nice
to feel the wind rush through your hair,
to feel your stomach flip
as you loop and gasp for air,

but I'd rather take the donkey ride,
a steady stroll along the beach,
with time for chips and sunsets
and hopes and plans and dreams,

time for ice creams and amusements
and to watch the waves for hours,
to know we'd be as happy
in Bali or at the Blackpool Tower.

So keep the roller coaster,
with its loops and dips and twists,
it's exciting for a short while,
but you can't stroll or kiss.

If I had the choice
I know exactly what I'd do,
I'd choose the donkey every time
and the beach, the chips and you.

COSMIC DUST

What a strange species we are,
buying houses, driving cars,
playing our roles,
stardust and souls,
in costumes of flesh and bone.
Pretending we know what's happening,
pretending we're not scared,
when really, we don't understand
a single thing,
and trying not to admit it's terrifying.
And so, we fill our baskets with biscuits,
our trolleys with tea,
hope and pray that no one can see.
I wish we could unzip our skins,
release our cosmic dust
and dance together,
forget about the shopping,
laugh at ourselves as we soar and play
amongst the stars
and live forever.

CRUMBLE AND CUSTARD

It was just crumble and custard,
but she made it so much more,
welcomed strangers as if old friends
arriving at her door.
My icy mood melted by her smile
as warm as the custard on top,
my bad mood gone,
crumbled in more ways than one.
I wondered how many lives she saves each day
ladling up that liquid sunshine?
A couple at least, filling up bellies and hearts
with warmth as they feast.
Each customer her favourite.
The real heroes walk among us,
ordinary people walking ordinary streets,
restoring faiths and repairing hearts
easily and without fuss.
Serving us and saving us,
one person at a time.
Serving up crumble and custard,
saving lives at six pounds a pop.
I'd have happily paid more
for extra custard on top.

… … BOOM! Out pops a big bang
creating everything, even us.
The stars are formed and explode,
we are all made from stardust,
we are all made from stars.

By Harry Cherry aged 9.

Printed in Great Britain
by Amazon